This book belongs to:

- -

- -

Enid Blyton's

The NEW Adventures of the

Wishing~Chair

Spellworld

Illustrated by Erica-Jane Waters

EGMONT

Special thanks to Narinder Dhami

EGMONT
We bring stories to life

The New Adventures of the Wishing-Chair: Spellworld
First published in Great Britain 2009
by Egmont UK Limited
239 Kensington High Street
London W8 6SA

ISBN 978 1 4052 4389 6

1 3 5 7 9 10 8 6 4 2

www.egmont.co.uk

A CIP catalogue record for this title
is available from the British Library

Printed and bound in Great Britain by Clays Ltd, St Ives plc

Contents

The Characters

Jack

Jessica

Mollie

Gertie

Wishler

Flick

'Look, Jessica!' Jack nudged his older sister. 'That one has got *huge* teeth!'

'He looks hungry,' Jessica commented. She threw another handful of fish food into the pond,

and the large golden fish that they'd

been watching greedily gobbled it

up. 'Mollie's garden is great, isn't it?'

Jessica went on, glancing around. Their neighbour's pond sat in the middle of a beautiful garden which was thick with flowers and shrubs.

Jack nodded and looked down at the gold, white and black fish that swam lazily round the little stone fountain in the water. 'I wonder if Mum and Dad would let *us* have a

pond?' he asked, looking across the fence at their own garden. 'We could make it ourselves. It'd be fun.'

'Maybe Wishler could help,' Jessica suggested with a wink. 'It would have to be at night though!'

Jack grinned. Their friend Wishler the pixie lived in the shed at the bottom of their garden along with

4

the magical wishing-chair, a special gift from a wizard who was called the Toymaker. No one could *ever* find out about Wishler or the wonderful adventures the three of them had when the wishing-chair took them to magical lands. Not even Jack and Jessica's mum and dad knew there was a pixie living in their shed!

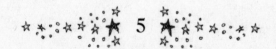 5

'That looks like thirsty work!' called
Mollie from the kitchen. 'How about
a glass of home-made lemonade?'

'Yes please,' Jessica
called back.
Mollie
came out
with a tray
of glasses.

'You'd better check that you've still got all your fingers,' she teased, handing round the lemonade. 'My fish are *very* greedy.'

Jack and Jessica laughed. Mollie wasn't like an old person at all, Jessica thought. She wore long, flowing skirts and jewelled flip-flops and lots of shining glass and amber beads

around her neck. She was always laughing and telling jokes, although Jessica had noticed that Mollie wasn't quite as cheerful this morning as she usually was.

'Thanks for helping me,' Mollie said gratefully. 'Tell me, how are you two enjoying living here in Noware?'

'It took a bit of getting used to,'

Jack replied, remembering how bored he and Jessica had been before they found the wishing-chair and Wishler. 'But now we love it!' He sipped on the lemonade. 'This is yummy. Are you going to serve some at your garden party tomorrow?'

Mollie's face fell a little.

'Are you OK?' Jessica asked Mollie

hesitantly. 'You seem a bit down in the dumps.'

Their neighbour sighed, and her blue eyes, which usually twinkled, were anxious. 'It's my roses,' she explained. 'Come and see.' She led Jack and Jessica over to a border full of rose bushes. 'My roses are always beautiful at this time of year,' she

said sadly. 'That's part of the reason why I have an annual garden party.'

Jack and Jessica nodded. They'd been invited, along with their parents.

'But my roses are dying.' Mollie sighed. 'I've tried everything I can think of to perk them up but nothing has worked.'

'They *do* look rather ill,' Jessica

admitted, staring at the pink, red and

white roses. The flower-heads were

drooping and the leaves looked brown and sickly.

'I guess I'll just have to go ahead with the garden party without my lovely roses,' Mollie said unhappily.

'Everyone will enjoy themselves anyway, especially with all of those cakes you've been baking,' Jack pointed out.

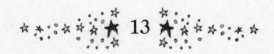

Mollie nodded, looking a tiny bit more cheerful.

Jack and Jessica finished their lemonade, said goodbye to Mollie and headed to the shed in their garden.

'I wish there was something we could do to help Mollie,' Jack said as they reached the shed door.

'Maybe Wishler can come up with

something,' Jessica suggested.

Wishler was busy dusting the shed when they went in. He looked very pleased to see them, his smile lighting up his little face. The wishing-chair stood in a corner of the shed, the colourful paintings that decorated its wooden frame glowing in the afternoon sunshine.

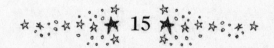

'Wishler, we need your help!' Jack announced. He quickly explained about Mollie's roses.

The pixie rubbed his chin. 'Well, whenever the Toymaker had a problem with his roses, he would

always use a *Get Better Spell*.'

'Can we get this spell for Mollie?' Jessica asked eagerly.

'Of course. We'll get the wishing-chair to take us to Spellworld,' Wishler replied. 'And when we get there, we'll catch the spell in a net!'

'Spellworld,' Jack repeated, wide-eyed with excitement. 'What's that?'

'Spellworld is the home of the *Which Witch Academy*,' Wishler explained. 'The trainee witches spend all day brewing new spells in their cauldrons. Sometimes these spells just drift out of the window and hang around in the air like clouds, until someone catches them and uses them up.'

'Someone like us!' Jessica clapped her hands in delight. 'How do you tell which spell is which?'

'First you have to find a spell that's the right colour, and then you taste it.' Wishler winked. 'Just a little bite, as you don't know what the spell is and anything might happen!'

'Let's go right away!' Jack yelled,

running over to the wishing-chair.

'This should be fun,' Wishler said as he, Jack and Jessica sat down on the seat of the chair. 'I haven't been spell-catching in years.'

The three of them rocked the wishing-chair back and forth. As they did so, blue sparks fizzed around the chair's rockers.

 20

'We wish to go to Spellworld!' Jessica shouted on the third rock.

Chapter
Two

There was a flash of blinding blue
light as the wishing-chair whizzed
up into the air and turned around.
Then, almost immediately, Jack and
Jessica felt the chair bump gently
down on the ground again.

Jessica blinked as the light began to clear. She was sitting on something rather squishy and lumpy.

'Jessica, get off!' Jack exclaimed. 'You're sitting on me.'

'And both of you are sitting on *me*!' Wishler wailed from the bottom of the heap.

'Sorry!' Jessica jumped to her

feet. As Jack and Wishler got up too,

she saw that the wishing-chair had

disguised itself as a small and delicate

silver stool.

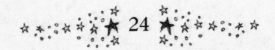

Jack looked around. They were inside a large old building with a tall, pointed roof, and they were surrounded by shelves filled with all kinds of objects, including jewelled sunglasses and silver binoculars. 'What is this place?' he asked.

'I think it's a shop,' Jessica replied. She pointed at the shelves nearest her which were filled with silver stools. 'The wishing-chair has disguised itself to fit in! Isn't it clever?'

Jack picked up one of the silver stools from the shelf. It had a golden tag tied to the leg.

'*Handcrafted by Bella the Witch,*'

Jack read aloud. '*Witchy surprise
included!*' He laughed. 'I wonder
what the surprise is?'

'The wishing-chair has got a tag

too,' Wishler pointed out.

Jessica looked at the tag. '*This stool is the property of Jack and Jessica,*' she read out. '*So keep your grubby hands off!*'

'The wishing-chair really likes you,' Wishler chuckled. 'It doesn't want to belong to anyone else.' He glanced over his shoulder. 'We're lucky that there was no one around to see us arrive. It's always very busy here.'

'Where are we, Wishler?' Jessica asked.

'A shop called *Spend a Spell*,' Wishler explained. 'And it has everything you need to have an exciting holiday in Spellworld.'

'Like binoculars,' Jack remarked,

wandering over to a nearby shelf.

'Those aren't just any old binoculars,' Wishler told him. 'They're for seeing falling stars!'

Jack put the binoculars to his eyes and gasped. All around him, silvery stars were falling to the ground. As Jack watched, a couple of stars floated down and landed on the pink

ribbon in Jessica's hair, but his sister didn't seem to notice. Jack took the binoculars away, and the stars disappeared.

'Follow me,' Wishler said, placing

the wishing-chair with the other silver stools. 'Aisle eight is where the spell-catching nets are kept.'

Aisle eight was the busiest in the whole shop. Jack and Jessica peered down it and saw lots of pixies, elves, centaurs and griffins swarming around the shelves. Fairies with glittery wings hovered overhead, and there were also young witches in long black cloaks among the crowd. They were all trying to grab one of the spell-catching nets.

'They look just like *our* fishing-nets,' Jack said to Jessica. 'The ones we take to Noware beach.'

'But ours aren't gold and silver!' Jessica pointed out.

The three friends waited patiently until at last they managed to reach the shelves. They chose golden nets with gleaming silver rods and joined the queue at the pay desk.

Jessica was just about to ask Wishler how they were going to pay,

when she heard a very familiar voice in front of them.

'Excuse me, I've been waiting *ages* . . .'

Jessica stood on tiptoe and peered over the heads of the shoppers in front.

'Do you have any Rainbow Roses for sale?' the voice went on.

At the head of the queue Jessica could see a young man with red hair, wearing a pointy green hat.

'It's Flick the wizard!' Jessica hissed to Wishler and Jack. 'I've got a few words to say to *him*!'

Chapter
Three

'Me too,' Jack agreed. 'I think it was pretty mean of him to give us pretend invisibility powder, *and* make a whole village of magical creatures ill!'

'He thinks it's funny to play pranks on people,' Jessica said. 'But I don't!'

'You should know better,' the bird-like shopkeeper was saying impatiently to Flick. 'Rainbow Roses can only be bought in special shops.' He pointed to the door at the back of the store. 'If you want one so much, you'd better search outside while it's still raining and before the last rainbow fades away. Next!'

Jack saw Flick trudge off gloomily. As the wizard approached the door he instantly spotted Jack, Jessica and Wishler in the queue.

'Hello!' Flick's face lit up. 'How nice to see you again!'

Jack, Jessica and Wishler just glared at him.

'Oh, I can see you're *still* mad

 about the pretend

invisibility powder.'

He looked sheepish.

'Sorry, it was just

a joke!'

'What about those chocolates that made everyone sick in the Land of Mythical Creatures?' Jessica asked crossly. 'Was *that* a joke too?'

Flick flushed red. 'I didn't know the chocolates were going to make the creatures sick,' he explained. 'I thought they were just going to give everyone hiccups.' He held out his hand. 'Friends?' he asked eagerly.

Jack, Jessica and Wishler glanced at each other. And they all nodded at the same time.

'Friends,' said Jack, shaking Flick's hand.

'But no more silly jokes,' Jessica warned in a stern voice.

'Sure,' Flick agreed. He looked at them curiously. 'What are you three doing in Spellworld?'

'We're looking for a *Get Better Spell*,' Wishler explained.

'I want a Rainbow Rose,' Flick sighed. 'But they don't have one.'

'What's a Rainbow Rose?' asked Jack curiously.

'It's an extremely powerful magical ingredient,' the wizard replied. 'Just one petal can really boost a spell's power! But they're so hard to find.' He frowned. 'I'd better get going.'

'Well, good luck,' said Jessica as they reached the front of the queue.

'Good luck to you too!' And Flick went off whistling.

'Now, then,' said the shopkeeper as he peered down at them. 'How will you pay for your nets?'

Jack pulled a few coins out of his pocket.

The shopkeeper shook his head and pointed at the ribbon in Jessica's hair. 'That will do nicely!'

'Sure,' Jessica agreed with a smile,

handing it over. 'I have lots more ribbons at home!'

Then, clutching their nets, the three of them hurried out of the shop

and into a village square alive with colours. It was still raining but Jack could tell that the raindrops weren't the same as the ones back home.

'Look at the *colours*!' Jessica exclaimed, blinking at the brightness all around them. 'It's like stepping inside a rainbow!'

Above them vivid, multi-coloured

clouds drifted across the sky, and there were huge rainbows arching here and there through them.

'And it's really weird, but the rain doesn't feel wet at all!' Jack added.

Holding out her hand, Jessica caught some of the gleaming drops. Instead of feeling wet, they were dry and tickled her palm like feathers.

Jessica could see that each drop was filled with tiny, sparkling rainbows of red, yellow, orange, indigo, blue, green and violet.

'Those coloured clouds are the spells,' Wishler explained. 'See how everyone is jumping around with their nets, trying to catch them?'

Jack and Jessica stared at the

creatures leaping up and down, trying to scoop spells up in their nets. Excitement flooded through them. They couldn't *wait* to join in and catch a spell of their own!

Chapter Four

'What colour is the *Get Better Spell*?' Jessica asked Wishler.

'Blue,' the pixie replied.

'There are *loads* of blue clouds!' Jack exclaimed. He could see shades of blue from aqua to indigo. 'How do

we know which one it is?'

Wishler scratched his head. 'I guess we'll have to taste them all,' he said. 'From what I remember our spell will taste like sherbet!'

'Yum!' Jessica laughed. 'But is it safe to taste lots of different spells?'

'As long as you only try a little bit, the spell won't last long,' Wishler

replied reassuringly.

Jack, Jessica and Wishler spotted a few low-hanging blue clouds and jumped up to catch them. Jessica soon realised that spell-catching was much harder than it looked because the clouds drifted this way and that, and some were very high up. Wishler was much better at it and managed

to catch a turquoise cloud in his net at just his third attempt.

'It looks like blue candy-floss,' Jack said, as Wishler took a small bite.

'This one tastes of apples –' the pixie began. There was a quick burst of turquoise smoke and Wishler vanished. A frog appeared instead and stared up at Jack and Jessica.

'*Ribbit!*' said the frog.

Jack and Jessica burst out laughing.

The frog disappeared with another

puff of smoke and Wishler was back. He shook his head. 'I'm glad that didn't last too long.'

The three friends began bounding around again with their nets.

'Got you!' Jack yelled loudly, capturing a sapphire-blue cloud. He nibbled at the fluffy edge and suddenly felt himself growing taller.

'What's happening?' he cried in a deep voice.

'Jack, you're all grown up!' Jessica giggled. 'You look exactly like Dad!' She bit off a piece of the same cloud, and felt herself growing taller too.

'Well, now you look like Mum!' Jack retorted, poking his tongue out at her cheekily.

Just as Jack and Jessica were shrinking back to their normal size, they had to duck as Wishler sailed over their heads in one huge bound.

'I've found a jumping spell!' Wishler called, holding out his net and showing them an azure-coloured cloud. 'It makes it easier to catch the other spells.'

Eagerly Jack and Jessica tasted tiny pieces of Wishler's cloud.

'Whee! Look at me!' Jack yelled as he soared up into the sky. Grinning, Jessica jumped off the ground too and shot upwards like a rocket.

'Don't catch any of the spells that are really high up!' Jessica heard Wishler call out anxiously. 'They're

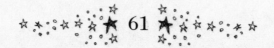

lighter than the others because they're unfinished. They can be very unpredictable!'

Jack landed on the ground and bounced upwards again, high into the air. He spotted a navy blue cloud and quickly netted it before he floated back down.

'Look,' Jack told Wishler excitedly.

'I've got a new cloud. It might be the *Get Better Spell*.'

'Did you hear what I said about unfinished spells?' Jessica heard Wishler say as she approached the ground, but she could tell that her brother wasn't listening. Jack nibbled at the navy blue cloud before Wishler could stop him.

'Ugh!' Jack scrunched up his face. 'It tastes really sour! Uh oh.' To Jack's dismay, he felt himself blowing up like a beach ball. As he did so, he immediately began to float up into the air.

'Jack!' Jessica shouted. 'Come back!' She grabbed her brother's leg to pull him down, but she was

instantly tugged off the ground as
well. She looked down at Wishler,
taking in his horrified gaze, as the
wind propelled her and her brother

away through the shower of rainbow drops.

'HELP!' Jack and Jessica screamed.

Chapter
Five

'Hold on!' Wishler called. Jack glanced

down and saw the pixie taste a little

more of the jumping spell, and then

come bounding after them.

In just a few moments, Jack and

Jessica had left the village square

behind and were floating over some green fields.

'Wishler, the spell isn't running out!' Jessica shouted.

'It must be an unfinished spell,' Wishler shouted back, leaping into the air next to them. 'I warned you they were unpredictable.'

Jessica could feel herself trembling

with fear as they floated higher, and her arms were aching as she held on tightly to Jack's leg. 'I hope we don't end up getting lost,' she called anxiously to Jack. 'And what if Wishler's spell runs out and he can't keep up with us?'

Nervously, Jack looked down. They were *really* sky high now. For a

second, his eye was
caught by a bright
flower nestling in
the grass below.
Even from this high up,
Jack could see that the flower
glowed with many different colours.

'I see someone!' Jessica shouted
suddenly. Up ahead, she spotted a

young witch wearing a black cape

and a pointed hat. She was peering

down at the grass with a magnifying-glass. Wishler bounded up into the air towards them again.

'Wishler, look – there's a witch.' Jessica pointed.

'Maybe she can help!' Jack said.

'Let's yell really loudly and get her attention,' Wishler suggested.

'HELP!' the three of them shrieked.

The witch glanced up. She grabbed

her broomstick from the grass, hopped on and soared up into the air towards them.

'Unfinished spell!' Wishler gasped, indicating Jack before dropping towards the ground again.

'Can you help?' Jessica asked the witch desperately.

'I'd be happy to.' The witch took

some purple powder from a leather

purse and blew it over Jack. Instantly,

he shrank down to his normal size,

but in the same moment he and

Jessica plummeted towards the ground like stones.

Jessica screamed as she saw the ground coming closer and closer. Quick as a flash the witch zoomed towards Jessica and Jack and caught them both on her broomstick. Feeling very shaky, Jessica and her brother clung on to the wooden handle of

the broom as the witch swooped

downwards and landed on the grass.

Wishler rushed to join them.

'Thank you!' the three friends chorused.

'You're welcome!' The witch smiled. 'I just used some undoing powder. It's very helpful when a spell goes wrong! I'm Gertie, by the way.'

'I'm Jessica, and this is Jack and Wishler,' Jessica said.

Wishler pointed at the magnifying-glass dangling from a cord on Gertie's wrist.

'What are you looking for?' he asked. 'We'd like to help if we can.'

'I'm searching for a Rainbow Rose,' Gertie explained. 'I have a big exam coming up at the academy, and a Rainbow Rose is essential for one of my spells!'

'Oh!' Jack exclaimed.

'I saw something

that looked like a

strange flower when

I was in the air. Its petals

were all different colours!'

'That sounds like a Rainbow Rose

all right!' Gertie said eagerly. 'Where

did you see it, Jack?'

Jack pointed across the field.

'Let's go and look!' Gertie cried.

They all ran across the field in the direction of the rose. But suddenly Wishler gave a shout. 'Oh no! It's Flick!'

'And he's heading straight towards the rose too!' Jessica cried.

Chapter
Six

Immediately Gertie handed her broomstick to Wishler and speeded up, leaving the pixie, Jessica and Jack behind.

'Wow, I knew witches were great sprinters, but Gertie's *really* fast!'

Wishler gasped out as they hurried after her.

'Looks like she's going to get to the rose first!' Jack panted.

Gertie was just about to pass a tall oak tree, when to Jessica's surprise the tree began to shake violently, even though there was no wind. Suddenly, a shower of acorns fell from the tree

on to the ground in front of the witch.

'Gertie, look out!' Jessica yelled. But it was too late. The witch's foot slipped on the acorns and she landed on her bottom with a thud.

Jack glanced at Flick. He was sure he saw the wizard tucking a green wand out of sight under his cloak as

he raced towards the Rainbow Rose.

'I think Flick made the acorns fall

on the ground!' Jack said, as he and

Jessica helped Gertie up.

'Ooh, that's not fair!' Gertie exclaimed, dashing off again.

'Hurry, Gertie!' Jessica called, as she, Jack and Wishler ran after her.

A few seconds later Flick reached the spot where Jack had seen the Rainbow Rose. But Gertie arrived at exactly the same moment. The two

of them stood nose to nose, glaring at each other fiercely.

'It's mine!' Flick declared. 'I got here first!'

'No, you didn't!' Gertie retorted. 'It was a draw!'

Wishler, Jack and Jessica joined them. Jessica glanced down and saw a beautiful rose nestled in the grass.

Its silky petals were all the colours
of the rainbow.

'The only fair way to settle this is to
have a contest,' Wishler said firmly.
'Whoever wins gets the rose.'

'Well, *I* got to the rose first and I'm
the smartest of you all, so I should set
the competition,' Flick argued sulkily.
'If none of you can answer this really

easy riddle, then the rose is mine,
Are we agreed?'

'You *didn't* get to the rose first
and you're certainly not smarter than
me,' Gertie said firmly. 'But we'll
answer your silly riddle.'

'Here it is then. What's the
difference between here and there?'
Flick asked, looking first over one

shoulder and then the other.

Jessica glanced two ways as Flick had just done. On one side was the oak tree, and on the other, nothing. Jessica frowned. The riddle was easy. Too easy!

She knew how much Flick liked playing pranks. This had to be a trick question! Suddenly the right answer

popped into Jessica's head. 'The letter *t*,' she said excitedly. 'That's the difference between here and there!'

Flick's face dropped in dismay.

'Well done, Jessica!' Jack said with a grin.

Jessica carefully picked the beautiful rose and handed it to Gertie. 'I believe this belongs to you.'

'I'll get you back for this,' Flick vowed crossly, and stomped off in a huff.

Chapter
Seven

'Don't worry about him,' Gertie said reassuringly. 'Everyone knows that Flick is full of hot air.' The young witch wrapped the rose carefully in a handkerchief. 'Thank you so much for this. Will you all come and have

tea with me at the academy?'

'Sorry, but we can't,' Jack said. 'We have to find a *Get Better Spell* and return home as soon as possible.'

'It's your lucky day! I've just brewed up a new batch of that very spell!' Gertie exclaimed. Pulling a blue bottle out of her pocket, she handed it to Jessica. 'Well, goodbye,' she said.

'Come and visit Spellworld again very soon!'

'We will,' Wishler promised. 'Goodbye Gertie! And thank you.'

Jack, Jessica and Wishler hurried back to *Spend a Spell*. The chair was still where they had left it, among the other silver stools.

'Show yourself,' Jack whispered.

There was a puff of blue smoke, the stool vanished and there was the wishing-chair. Jessica, Jack and Wishler sat down.

'Home!' Jessica shouted, as the three of them began to rock.

Sparks flew around the chair and in a flash, they were back in the shed at the bottom of the garden.

'What a great adventure!' Jack exclaimed. 'But how are we going to use the *Get Better Spell* on the roses without Mollie knowing?'

Jessica peeked out of the shed window and saw Mollie setting out chairs in her lawn in preparation for tomorrow's garden party. 'Let's go and offer to help,' she suggested. 'We might get a chance to use the spell.'

'I'd like to help, but I'll have to stay here,' Wishler said with a sigh. 'She mustn't see me!'

Waving goodbye to Wishler, Jack and Jessica hurried next door and offered their assistance.

'Well, it *is* very kind of you to help me twice in one day!' Mollie exclaimed. 'I have some more chairs in the house to bring outside.'

'I'll get them,' Jack said quickly.

Jessica hung back while Jack

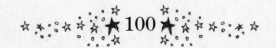

and Mollie went inside. Then she

uncorked the blue bottle and began

sprinkling the *Get Better Spell* on the

rose trees. The drops of liquid fizzed slightly as they fell on the petals, and then vanished.

'Did you use the spell?' Jack whispered as he came back, carrying a chair.

Jessica nodded. 'I hope it works. Let's see how they look tomorrow . . .'

Next morning, Jack and Jessica were up bright and early. They ran out to the garden and peered eagerly over the fence.

'Look, Jessica!' Jack cried in delight. 'The spell worked!'

Jessica could see that the roses were blooming beautifully

and the leaves looked fresh and healthy. Mollie was in her kitchen and she waved to Jack and Jessica from the window.

'My roses are lovely again, aren't they?' she called with a smile. 'Wait there, I have some blueberry muffins for you!'

'Oh, yum!' Jessica said as Mollie came out with a plate. 'Three muffins!'

'They're to say thank you for helping

me yesterday,' Mollie explained. 'There's one for you, one for Jack and one for your little friend with the green hat who lives in the shed.'

Jack and Jessica looked at each other in complete horror. How had Mollie found out about Wishler?

Chapter Eight

'Don't look so worried,' Mollie said quickly, 'I promise I won't tell anyone. It'll be our secret.' She looked at Jack and Jessica with twinkling blue eyes. 'Besides, you might be interested to know that when I was a girl, my

brother Peter and I had a little friend too, who hid in our playroom at the bottom of our garden!'

'You mean like Wishler?' Jessica gasped.

Mollie nodded. 'We also had a magical wishing-chair,' she said dreamily. 'The chair had wings, and it used to take the three of us to

wonderful lands where we had many

marvellous adventures!'

Jack and Jessica could hardly believe their ears.

'We have a wishing-chair too!' Jack could hardly get the words out, he was so amazed. 'But it doesn't have wings, it has rockers –'

'Jack!' Jessica squealed excitedly. 'Remember what Wishler said about the wishing-chair? He said that the

Toymaker put rockers on it because its wings were damaged!'

'Well!' Mollie looked just as excited as Jessica. 'It sounds like it might be the same wishing-chair. How strange that I've ended up living next door to it!' She grinned at Jack and Jessica. 'But then magic works in mysterious ways, doesn't it? I'm so glad you and

your little friend are having such great adventures!'

Jack and Jessica beamed at her. Just then they heard their mother calling from the kitchen.

'Jack, Jessica! We're going shopping in ten minutes.'

'We have to go, Mollie,' Jessica said, 'but we'll see you later at the party.'

'Don't forget the muffin for Wishler!' Mollie handed them the plate across the fence. 'And some day

soon, you must *all* come over and I'll tell you about my wishing-chair adventures.'

'That'd be great!' Jack said, as Mollie waved and went inside.

'Quick, Jack, let's go and give Wishler his muffin,' Jessica said. 'I can't wait to tell him that Mollie used to own the wishing-chair!'

'I can't wait to hear all about Mollie's adventures,' Jack added eagerly, '*and* to find out where the wishing-chair will take us next time!'

EGMONT PRESS: ETHICAL PUBLISHING

Egmont Press is about turning writers into successful authors and children into passionate readers – producing books that enrich and entertain. As a responsible children's publisher, we go even further, considering the world in which our consumers are growing up.

Safety First
Naturally, all of our books meet legal safety requirements. But we go further than this; every book with play value is tested to the highest standards – if it fails, it's back to the drawing-board.

Made Fairly
We are working to ensure that the workers involved in our supply chain – the people that make our books – are treated with fairness and respect.

Responsible Forestry
We are committed to ensuring all our papers come from environmentally and socially responsible forest sources.

For more information, please visit our website at www.egmont.co.uk/ethical